For Ben and Tom, with love
J.W

For little John and Pauline, with love
T.B.

First published in Great Britain in 2006 by Gullane Children's Books
This paperback edition published in 2007 by
Gullane Children's Books
185 Fleet Street, London EC4A 2HS
www.gullanebooks.com

3 5 7 9 10 8 6 4

Text © Julia Rawlinson 2006
Illustrations © Tiphanie Beeke 2006

The right of Julia Rawlinson and Tiphanie Beeke to be identified as the author and illustrator of this work
has been asserted by them in accordance with the Copyright, Designs and Patents Act, 1988.
A CIP record for this title is available from the British Library.

ISBN: 978-1-86233-679-7

Printed and bound in China

This book belongs to

_____

Ferdie
and the
Falling
Leaves

Julia Rawlinson • Tiphanie Beeke

GULLANE
CHILDREN'S BOOKS

The world was changing. Each morning, when Ferdie
bounced out of the den, everything seemed just a little bit different.
The rich green of the forest was turning to a dusty gold, and the
soft swishing sound of summer was fading to a crinkly whisper.
Ferdie's favourite tree was looking dull, dry and brown.

Ferdie, visiting it every day, was
beginning to get worried.

"I think my tree is ill," said Ferdie.
"What's wrong with it?" asked Mummy.
"Its leaves are turning brown," said Ferdie.
"Don't worry, it's only autumn," smiled Mummy.

Ferdie trotted back to his
tree and patted the rough bark.
"Don't worry, it's only autumn,"
he said. "You'll soon be feeling better."

But the tree didn't get better. Day
by day, it got browner still. One day, as
Ferdie sat under the tree, the wind began
to blow. A small brown leaf blew off
the tree and drifted towards the ground. Ferdie
jumped up and caught it, very gently, in his paw.

"Don't worry, tree, I've got your leaf. You'll soon be fixed," said Ferdie. He looked around, scratched his head and picked a piece of grass. He carefully tied the leaf to its branch and sat happily down.

Just then another gust of wind ruffled Ferdie's fur. The little leaf shook itself free and fluttered back to the ground.

Ferdie picked it up again and thought very hard. Then he poked the leaf onto a twig and pushed it firmly down. "Now you hold on tight," said Ferdie, sternly. "No more flying around." The little leaf gave a tiny rustle in reply.

The next day a strong wind
was blowing through the forest.
Ferdie rushed out of the den and ran all the
way to his tree. Lots of its branches were brown
and bare and little lost leaves whirled everywhere.
"Don't worry, tree," he called in alarm,
"I'll catch them for you, I promise."

Round and round and round whirled Ferdie, after the twirling leaves.

"Leaves! Wonderful! Just
what I need for my nest,"
said a squirrel, scampering up.
"But these belong to the tree,"
said Ferdie, "don't take these away."
"The tree doesn't need them any more,"
said the squirrel, and off he bounded.

"Help! Help! The wind and the squirrel
are stealing our leaves," cried a frantic Ferdie.

"Leaves! Marvellous! Just what I need to
keep warm," said a hedgehog, rolling around.

"But these belong to the tree," said Ferdie,
plucking leaves from the hedgehog's prickles.
"Not any more," snuffled the hedgehog, and away he rolled.
"Help! The wind, the squirrel and the hedgehog are
stealing our leaves," cried a frenzied Ferdie.

This time, a flock of friendly birds
swooped down from the sky. They
picked the leaves up in their beaks and
poked them onto the tree's branches.
Soon the tree was leafy again, and
Ferdie flopped down and smiled.

"Thank you, thank you, birds,"
he gasped, as the birds fluttered
and chirruped away. He lay, looking
up through the leaves at the sky,
and drifted off to sleep.

But still the wind continued to blow, and still the branches danced.

The leaves shivered and shook themselves

and began to wriggle free.

They tossed and turned

and twitched and twirled

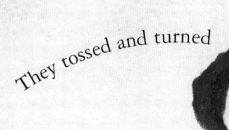

and tumbled to the ground.

They brushed Ferdie's ears and nose

and filled his dreams with a whispering sound.

When Ferdie finally blinked awake, he couldn't believe his eyes.
Instead of a roof of dancing leaves, he could see bare branches
against the sky. "Oh tree, I am so sorry," gulped Ferdie.
"All your leaves are gone."
But then he saw, high in the branches,
one small leaf still holding on.

"I won't let the wind steal that one,"
said Ferdie, and he began to climb.

He wriggled along
to the last leaf and held
it firmly onto its branch.

All day long the wind
blew, the branch bounced
and Ferdie held tight.
"I'll stay with you, leaf," he
gasped. "Don't worry that
all your friends have gone."

But then with a sudden whoosh of wind the
branch bounced high. With a whispered PLIP!
the leaf let go and fluttered like a
little flag, clutched in Ferdie's paw.

Ferdie looked sadly at the leaf, the tree's last
leaf he had promised to save. He carried it carefully
down the tree and all the way back to the den.

He made it a cosy little bed and gently
tucked it in for the night, but all night long he
could only think of his tree, all on its own.

At first light he tiptoed out into the chilly dawn.
The wind had finally stopped blowing and the air
was damp and cold. The moon still hung in
the clear sky and pale stars glimmered.

As he came to his favourite tree,
Ferdie saw a magical sight . . .

The tree was hung with a thousand icicles, shining silver in the early light. "You are more beautiful than ever," whispered Ferdie to the tree made of ice. "Can the squirrel and the hedgehog keep your leaves for the cold winter nights?"

A tiny breeze shivered the branches, making a sound like laughter, and in the light of the rising sun the sparkling branches nodded.

Other Ferdie Books for you to enjoy

Ferdie's Springtime Blossom

When Ferdie tumbles down the hill into the sunny orchard, he can hardly believe his eyes – there's snow on the ground! Off he rushes to warn his friends that spring hasn't yet arrived. But could there be another explanation for the glorious white display?

'Captivating'
PUBLISHERS WEEKLY (STARRED REVIEW)

'Beeke – definitely a talent to watch out for!'
THE SCHOOL LIBRARIAN

* * *

Ferdie's Christmas

It's Christmas Eve and Ferdie has had a terrible thought – what if Father Christmas can't find the rabbits' new burrowto deliver their presents? Luckily Ferdie has an idea and he and his friends set about making Christmas perfect. . .

'Colorful warm pastel illustrations fill each page and evoke the spirit of the season'
SCHOOL LIBRARY JOURNAL

'Rawlinson's descriptions are transporting'
THE HORN BOOK

'Richly satisfying'
BOOKLIST